Help! There's a Ghost in My Room!

Dear Michelle,

My brother and I are arguing.
Is candy corn orange with da white stripe?
Or white with an orange stripe?

From,
Puzzled

Dear Michelle,
Help! My teacher spits
when he talks. And
I sit in the front
row! How can I get
him to stop?

From,
Say it. Don't
spray it!

Dear Michelle,
My cat has the worst
breath. When she says
Mew, I say P.U.
What should I do?

From,
Grossed Out

Help! There's a Ghost in My Room!

by Judy Katschke

HarperEntertainment
An Imprint of HarperCollinsPublishers

A PARACHUTE PRESS BOOK

A PARACHUTE PRESS BOOK

Parachute Publishing, L.L.C.
156 Fifth Avenue
Suite 302
New York, NY 10010

Published by

☰HarperEntertainment

An Imprint of HarperCollins*Publishers*
10 East 53rd Street, New York, NY 10022-5299

ISBN 0-06-054083-4

First printing: September 2003

Printed in the United States of America

Visit HarperEntertainment on the World Wide Web at
www.harpercollins.com

10 9 8 7 6 5 4 3 2 1

Chapter One

"Maybe we'll have recess the whole day!" I said. "Or pepperoni pizza and cotton candy for lunch!"

It was Monday morning. All the kids in my third-grade class were gathered by the blackboard. That's because our teacher, Mrs. Ramirez, had written the words *Big Surprise Today* in huge letters on it. I didn't have a clue what the big surprise was. But it was fun to guess!

"Or maybe we're getting a brand-new school bus!" I said to my best friends, Mandy Metz and Cassie Wilkins.

"Yeah!" Mandy cheered. "With built-in TV sets and bubblegum machines!"

"Or maybe—" I started to guess again.

Julia Rossi shoved between Cassie and me. "Quit guessing," she said. "Because *I* know what the surprise is."

"Here we go again," I said.

Julia "Bossy" Rossi thought she knew everything. But she didn't. Just last week she got the word *pumpkin* wrong on our spelling test.

"So what's the surprise?" I asked her.

"We're getting another class pet," Julia said.

"What kind?" Louie Rizzoli asked. "A guinea pig? A snake?"

"*Wrong*," Julia said. Then she looked at Cassie. She smiled one of her really mean smiles. "We're getting another *gerbil*!"

"No!" Cassie moaned. "Not another one!"

Cassie was afraid of our class gerbil,

Swifty. I knew Julia said that just to scare her silly!

"Okay, boys and girls!" Mrs. Ramirez said. Her long, curly brown hair was held back with a silver clip. And she was always wearing fun earrings. Today she had on dangly ones shaped like pumpkins.

Mrs. Ramirez gave the class a friendly smile. "The quicker you get to your seats, the quicker you'll find out what the big surprise is!"

All eighteen of us raced to our desks. Mine is the third desk in the third row. It's close enough to the window to feel a breeze on a nice day. And close enough to the closet to smell the rubber boots when it rains!

"Class, are you ready to find out what the surprise is?" Mrs. Ramirez asked with a grin.

"Yes!" we all shouted.

"We're going to start a class newspaper," Mrs. Ramirez announced. "And we're going to put it out once a month."

The class hummed with excitement.

"Cool!" Louie cried. "I'll get to be a reporter, just like my dad!"

Wow! I thought. We have our own class table in the lunchroom. And a class candy jar for rewarding good behavior. Even a class pet. But a class newspaper is huge!

"Any questions?" Mrs. Ramirez asked.

"Ooh! Ooh! Ooh!" Gracie Chin called out. She never raised her hand without yelling *Ooh! Ooh! Ooh!*

"Yes, Gracie?" Mrs. Ramirez asked.

"What's the newspaper called?" Gracie gasped. She was always out of breath when she finally asked her question.

"That's where I need your help," Mrs. Ramirez told us. "Can anyone in the class come up with a name for our newspaper?"

Someone called out *Third-Grade Scoop.* But everyone thought that sounded like an ice-cream parlor. Someone else yelled out *The Class Report,* but that made everyone think of report cards!

Come on, brain. I tapped my head. Think of something!

"Anybody else?" Mrs. Ramirez asked. She looked around the classroom. "I can hear you all buzzing about it."

Buzzing . . . Buzz . . . That's it!

I raised my hand. "How about the *Third-Grade Buzz*?" I asked.

"I like it!" Mandy cried.

"Me too!" Cassie said.

"Me three!" Jeff Farrington added.

Everyone laughed.

"The *Third-Grade Buzz,*" Mrs. Ramirez repeated. "What a good title. Thank you, Michelle."

Julia turned around in the seat in

front of me. "The *Buzz*? That makes us sound like a bunch of bees!"

Mrs. Ramirez waited for us to quiet down. Then she went on. "Our class will be putting together the *Third-Grade Buzz*," she explained. "But *all* the classes at Fraser Elementary will get to read it."

Manuel Martinez raised his hand. "The fifth grade too?" he asked.

"That's right!" Mrs. Ramirez said.

"But, Mrs. Ramirez," Elizabeth cried out. "How are we going to do our homework and write the newspaper both at the same time?"

Elizabeth's last name was Weaner. But secretly everyone called her *whiner*. That's because she was always complaining and worrying about something.

"The news stories will be *part* of your homework," Mrs. Ramirez explained.

Jamar's hand shot up. "Mrs. Ramirez,

my dad caught a shark over the weekend," he said. "Is that news?"

"It sure is, Jamar," Mrs. Ramirez said. "Now, the *Buzz* will come out once a month," she repeated. "So I'll need volunteers to write the monthly columns."

"Ooh! Ooh! Ooh!" Gracie called, raising her hand. "Mrs. Ramirez! Mrs. Ramirez!"

"Yes, Gracie?" Mrs. Ramirez asked.

"What's a column?" Gracie asked.

"A column is a piece of writing that appears in a newspaper," Mrs. Ramirez explained. "It is written by the same person every time. So whoever writes one will have his or her name in *our* newspaper every month!"

"That's so cool!" I whispered to Mandy. She was sitting at the desk on my left.

I really hoped I'd get picked to write a column. My whole family would be so proud. And in my full house that's a lot of people.

There's my dad, Danny, and my two older sisters, D.J. and Stephanie. My mom died when I was little, so Joey Gladstone moved in to help take care of us. He's my dad's best friend from college. And that's not all!

My uncle, Jesse, moved in too. And he got married to Aunt Becky. Then they had twin boys, Nicky and Alex. And that's *still* not all.

Finally there's our dog, Comet. He would be proud too if I wrote a newspaper column. Well, he would if he could read!

"We'll start with the joke-of-the-month column," Mrs. Ramirez said. "Who wants to write that one?"

A bunch of hands went up. So did mine.

I know a lot of funny jokes, I thought. And Uncle Joey tells jokes for a living! He could help me. And if I chewed tons of bubblegum, I could get all those jokes on the wrappers! I could—

"Jeff, I would like you to write the joke

column," Mrs. Ramirez told Jeff Farrington in the second row. "I'm sure you have lots of funny jokes you can share with us."

Jeff nodded. "Yeah, like what do cows do when they're not making milk?" He didn't even wait for an answer. "They go to the moooooovies!"

I laughed. Jeff was the class clown. No wonder Mrs. Ramirez picked him! I gave Jeff the thumbs-up sign.

"Next is the sports column," Mrs. Ramirez said. "So whoever writes it must like sports."

A bunch of hands shot up again. I raised my hand too.

I'm on the soccer team! I thought. I eat cereal that has an athlete's picture on the box! I watch football on TV with my dad and Uncle Jesse! I—

"Bailey?" Mrs. Ramirez asked. "How about you?"

"Sure!" Bailey said.

My hand dropped again. Bailey Zimmerman was the fastest runner and highest jumper in the class. She was also our secret weapon when it came to field day. No wonder Mrs. Ramirez had picked her!

"Congratulations," I whispered to Bailey.

"The next column is extra special," Mrs. Ramirez explained.

Come on, hand! I wiggled all five fingers. Don't let me down!

"It's called an advice column," Mrs. Ramirez went on. "The student who writes it will answer letters from kids with questions or problems."

Letters? I *love* getting letters!

My hand popped up so fast I almost fell off my seat. But Julia's hand went up too. We stretched higher and higher until we were both standing up!

Julia tried to jump in front of me. She

even yelled out, "Ooh! Ooh! Ooh!" just like Gracie.

"Michelle Tanner?" Mrs. Ramirez asked. "How would you like to write your own advice column?"

"You bet I would!" I cried. "Thanks, Mrs. Ramirez!"

I couldn't believe it. I was going to have my own column every month! I wanted to do a million cartwheels all around the school and all the way home. But I didn't.

"It's not fair," Julia grumbled to me. "You got to name the paper. And now you get a column too!"

But everyone else was smiling at me!

"Yay, Michelle!" Paige Alexander waved her feathery pink pen in the air.

"Very nice, Michelle," Sergei Petrovich said from across the aisle. Sergei was new and from Russia. He hasn't learned sayings like *congratulations* or *way to go* yet.

"Thanks, Sergei," I told him.

"That's it for the columns, boys and girls," Mrs. Ramirez said. "I want you all to start thinking about news stories. And some of you can draw pictures for the paper if you'd like."

I started thinking right away. I was already making plans. Big, big plans!

I would make a letter box in arts and crafts today. And decorate it with glitter and paper stars. And I'd hang it right outside the classroom where everyone could see it—even the fifth graders.

And I'd call it . . .

Dear Michelle!

Chapter Two

"Check it out!" I said to Cassie and Mandy the next morning at school. "I hung up my letter box yesterday afternoon. And it's already packed with letters!"

Cassie jumped up and down. "How many did you get, Michelle?"

"Let's see," I said. I gave my box a couple of shakes. Then I placed it on my desk. "Sounds like three letters."

"Or four!" Mandy said. "Give it another shake, Michelle."

I did.

Mandy nodded. "Definitely four."

"Wowie!" Cassie said. "Open the box and read them, Michelle. Pleeeeease?"

Elizabeth and Jamar came over to watch. So did Olivia Jackson and Lauren Kubo.

"Here goes." I rolled up the sleeves of my red-and-white striped sweater. Then I stuck my hand through the letter slot. And pulled out—

"A gum wrapper?" I held up a ball of crinkled foil. "This is a mailbox, not a garbage can."

Olivia and Lauren giggled.

"Try again, Michelle," Mandy said.

"Okay." I dug into my letter box. This time I pulled out a piece of paper.

"Looks like a letter to me!" Jamar said.

"Me too!" I started to read it and groaned. "Give me a break," I said. "This is Jeff's math homework."

Jeff snickered from somewhere in the classroom.

"Ha ha," I called out. "Very funny, Jeff!"

I was about to dig in for the third time when Elizabeth poked my arm. "Michelle, what if you *never* find a letter in your box?" she asked. "What if all you find are soggy tuna-fish sandwiches? Or Spencer Ericksen's tissues? Or something messy from Swifty's cage? Or—"

"Quit it, Elizabeth!" Mandy cut in. "There's got to be a letter in there somewhere!"

I stuck my hand in again. This time I pulled out a white piece of paper. It had a pretty flower design around the edges. And the words *Dear Michelle* were written at the top!

"It's a letter!" I cheered. I began reading it out loud. "'Dear Michelle'—"

"Dear Michelle! Dear Michelle!" Julia repeated in a mean voice. She was standing between Jamar and Olivia. Her arms were folded across her chest. "I should have been picked for the advice column. Not you!"

"Says who?" Cassie asked.

"Says *me!*" Julia pointed to herself. "I'm always giving advice to my little brother. Like the time he wanted to throw out his toy turtle. I told him to flush it down the toilet—and it came up in the bathtub!"

"That's not good advice," I said. "The turtle could have gotten stuck in the pipes."

Julia shrugged. "Well, if you think you can do better, let's hear *your* great advice," she said.

"No problem," I said. I held up the pretty letter and read it out loud. "'Dear Michelle, Help! I just moved into a creepy old house and it's totally haunted. I hear the ghost thumping around at night when everybody else is sleeping. One time it sounded like it was in my room! I'm really scared.

What should I do? From, Ghost Girl.'"

"Oh, boy," Jamar said. "That's a tough one."

"So, *Dear Michelle*." Julia put her hands on her hips. "What's your answer?"

Everybody stared at me, waiting.

I thought for a second. Two seconds. Three. Then I remembered what my dad once told me when I was little—when I thought there was a ghost in my closet.

"I know!" I gave Julia my biggest grin. "There are no such things as ghosts!"

Julia blinked. "Huh?"

"That's my answer," I told her. "There are no such things as ghosts. Period."

Julia made a huffy sound. "Well, *I* would have told Ghost Girl to hide under the covers. Because ghosts can't get you under there," she said.

"So that means *you* believe in ghosts," I said. "Right?"

"I do not!" Julia said. Then she pushed past me to her desk.

"You showed her, Michelle," Cassie said.

"Not only that," Mandy said, "you answered your first letter!"

"I know," I said, smiling. "Writing the 'Dear Michelle' column is going to be fun!"

Chapter Three

"Today we're going to read our first columns out loud to the class," Mrs. Ramirez said Thursday morning.

I bounced in my seat. I had read Ghost Girl's letter two whole days ago. And I worked really hard on my answer to her. I wanted to get it just right. I even typed it up on my family's computer. I couldn't wait to read my answer to the class!

I hope Mrs. R picks me to go first! I thought.

"Jeff?" Mrs. Ramirez asked. "Would you like to read your joke for our newspaper?"

I sank back in my chair.

"Okay, Mrs. Ramirez." Jeff stood up. "'Why didn't the skeleton cross the road?'" He looked around the room. When no one answered, he said. "'Because he didn't have any guts!'"

Jeff cracked up at his own joke. So did the rest of the class. It *was* pretty funny.

"Good one, Jeff!" Mrs. Ramirez said, laughing. "And just in time for Halloween."

Jeff crossed his eyes and took a bow. Then he sat in his seat.

"And now we'll hear from . . ." Mrs. Ramirez looked around the room.

Me, me, me! I thought.

". . . Bailey," Mrs. Ramirez said.

I slouched back again.

Bailey jumped up from her seat. She read all about the dodgeball game in the school yard. And how Jamar threw the ball right through Principal Posey's window!

"It was an accident!" Jamar shouted. "I was aiming for Sergei and he ducked."

"Thank you, Bailey," Mrs. Ramirez told her. "But remember to write that Jamar didn't mean it. Okay?"

"Okay, Mrs. Ramirez." Bailey sat down.

Then I finally heard the words I was waiting for.

"Michelle," Mrs. Ramirez said, "you're next."

I stood and read the letter from Ghost Girl. Then I read my answer:

"Dear Ghost Girl,

One night I thought I heard a ghost in my house. But it turned out to be the big grandfather clock in the hall.

I bet what you think is a ghost is something else too. Maybe the noise is your mom or dad walking to the kitchen for a glass of water. Or maybe it could be a tree branch hitting your window.

Whatever it is, don't worry. There are no such things as ghosts.

And that's my answer.

> *Love,*
> *Michelle"*

"Yeah, right," I heard Julia whisper.

But when I looked up from my paper, Mrs. Ramirez was smiling! "That was a very good answer, Michelle," she said. "And very helpful to Ghost Girl."

"Thank you, Mrs. Ramirez."

Hooray! I thought as I sat in my seat. Mrs. Ramirez liked my letter. So Ghost Girl probably will too. Whoever she is!

Suddenly Spencer tossed something onto my desk. It was a note folded into a tiny triangle.

"It's from Shelby," Spencer whispered.

"Thanks, Spencer," I whispered back.

Shelby Warner had brown hair, brown eyes, and freckles on her nose. She had just moved to San Francisco. I didn't know her very well yet. But she seemed nice.

I unfolded the note. Then I read it to myself. It said:

> *Michelle,*
> *I am Ghost Girl!*
> *Shelby W.*

"Wow!" I said under my breath. "Cool!"

I tore a piece of paper from my notebook and wrote a note to her:

> *Shelby,*
> *Did you like my answer?*
> *Love,*
> *Michelle*

23

I folded up the paper and passed it to Spencer.

Then Spencer passed it to Shelby.

Shelby opened the note and read it. And I waited for her reply. Well? What did she think? Did she like it?

Shelby looked at me, but she didn't smile. Instead she stuck her hand into the aisle and gave me a big thumbs-down!

Uh-oh, I thought. That means . . . *no*!

"I don't know why Shelby didn't like my answer," I told Cassie and Mandy at recess. We were hanging upside down on the monkey bars. A dodge ball rolled past us.

"So why don't you ask her?" Cassie said.

"Good idea," I said.

Shelby was walking toward us. Was she smiling or frowning? It was hard to tell upside down!

Cassie, Mandy, and I climbed off the

monkey bars. Shelby came by and grabbed the dodge ball.

"Hey, Shelby," I said. "How come you didn't like my answer?"

Shelby looked over her shoulder. Then she took a few steps closer to us. "Because ghosts *are* real," she said. "Ever since we moved to our new house I've been hearing these weird noises every night. And it's *not* a clock."

"Did you tell your mom and dad?" I asked.

Shelby nodded. "They say there's got to be a reason for the noises," she said. "But I know the reason—ghosts. And if you don't believe me you can all come to my house and see for yourself."

That sounded like a good idea to me. "We'll come to your house, Shelby. And then we'll see what's really making those strange noises," I said. "Where do you live?"

"I live at 1515 Hummingbird Lane," Shelby answered.

"Okay. We'll be there," I told Shelby.

"We *cannot* go *there*," Mandy said after Shelby left us. "Shelby's house is the creepy old house on the hill that everybody says is haunted."

"I heard that stuff in that house flies around all by itself," Cassie said. "And my brother said that one time he saw it raining on that house—but everywhere else it was sunny!"

I knew about the haunted house on Hummingbird Lane too. It was old and really scary-looking. And there were lots of creepy stories about it.

"But we don't know if those stories are true," I said.

"I don't care," Cassie whispered. "I'm scared of that place, Michelle!"

Cassie was scared of *a lot* of things:

creepy movies, the dark, windup toys that spit sparks—even colorful Gummi Worms!

But I wasn't afraid. I didn't believe in ghosts. And I didn't believe in haunted houses!

"Just because Shelby's house *looks* haunted doesn't mean it *is* haunted," I told my friends. "There are no such things as ghosts. And I'm going to prove it!"

Chapter Four

"There it is!" Shelby said when we reached Hummingbird Lane after school. She pointed to the towering gray house at the top of the hill. "That's where I live."

Cassie, Mandy, and I followed Shelby up the street and into her front yard.

"I saw a movie about a haunted house on TV once," Mandy whispered. "And the ghosts walked right through walls."

"Cut it out, Mandy," Cassie said. "I'm scared!"

I had to admit it. I was a little scared too. The grass in the yard was so high it reached my knees. The trees had no leaves—just branches that looked like skinny fingers.

A cackling crow flew over our heads, and I gulped. The closer we got to Shelby's house, the creepier it looked!

The gray paint on the house was cracked and peeling. The number 1515 hung on the door. But the second 5 swung back and forth on a rusty nail.

"So?" Shelby asked as we climbed onto the creaky porch. "What do you think of my house?"

Cassie and Mandy stared at me.

What did I think? I thought Shelby's house looked like every haunted house I had ever seen in scary movies! But I tried to sound cheerful.

"All it needs is a little paint," I said, smiling. "My dad is a total clean freak. Maybe he could help you fix it up!"

"Just wait." Shelby sighed. She used the brass knocker on the door. It was shaped like a pig's head.

A few seconds later Shelby's mom opened the door. She had short brown hair like Shelby's. But no freckles.

"Hi, kids!" Mrs. Warner gave us a big, friendly smile.

I smiled back. Shelby's mom seemed pretty nice. There was nothing creepy about her!

"Mom, this is Michelle, Cassie, and Mandy," Shelby said. "They're in my class."

"Come in," Mrs. Warner said. "I just baked a fresh batch of cookies!"

Shelby led us into the house. There were colorful rugs on the floor. And paintings of flowers, cats, and beaches all over the walls.

Nothing creepy about the inside, I thought.

"I hope you like chocolate chips."

Shelby tossed her red hoodie onto a chair in the front hallway. "My mom makes awesome chocolate chip cookies."

"Yum!" I said. There was nothing creepy about chocolate chip cookies either!

We followed Mrs. Warner into the kitchen. A boy with brown hair was sitting at the table. He was wearing a softball mitt on one hand. His other hand was stuffing cookies into his mouth.

"That's my little brother, Rufus," Shelby said. "He's six."

"Six and a *half*!" Rufus said, smiling. His teeth were covered with chocolate. "And I play softball!"

Meow!

Cassie gasped as a black cat jumped onto the table.

"That's Inky," Shelby explained.

"Hi, Inky!" I scratched him behind his ears. "You're really cute!" But not as cute as

31

my dog, Comet, I thought. I kept that part to myself.

Mrs. Warner poured us each a glass of milk. Then she ruffled Rufus's hair and said, "Come on, Rufus. Let's go to the den and work on those clay dinosaurs!"

Mrs. Warner and Rufus left the kitchen.

I plucked a chocolate chip out of my cookie and popped it into my mouth. "There is nothing spooky about your house, Shelby," I said. "I don't see or hear any ghosts anywhere."

Shelby leaned across the table and whispered, "That's because they don't come out in the daytime. They only come out at night."

"Did you see them?" I asked.

"I never really *saw* them," Shelby admitted. She leaned over even more. "But late at night when everyone is asleep I hear things. *Weird* things."

"What weird things?" I didn't mean for my voice to squeak, but it did.

"Sometimes I hear the TV and radio go on and off when there's nobody downstairs!" Shelby said.

"Maybe it's your mom," I guessed. "Maybe she watches TV when she can't sleep."

Shelby shook her head. "I peek into my parents' room after the noises start," she said. "And they're always fast asleep!"

"Oh," I said.

"And a couple of times I heard someone out in the hallway," Shelby said. "Right outside my door!"

"Did you look to see who it was?" I asked.

"No way!" Shelby cried.

"I wouldn't look either," Mandy admitted.

"Me neither!" Cassie agreed.

"And one morning," Shelby went on, "I

found a chicken drumstick on the stairs! What do you think of that?"

"I didn't know ghosts liked chicken," I joked.

But nobody laughed—or even smiled.

"Shelby, there's got to be a reason for all that stuff," I said. "It can't be a ghost. It just can't be."

"That's what you think," Shelby said. "I wish you could come over at night so you could hear for yourself."

"Me too. But I'm not allowed to go anywhere alone after dark," I said. "Well, except to a sleepover."

Shelby's eyes lit up. "Why don't you sleep here Saturday night? I'd get to have my first sleepover in our new house," she said. "It would be so cool!"

"Awesome!" I told Shelby. "But first I have to ask my dad, okay?"

"Okay!" Shelby said. She looked across

34

the table at Cassie and Mandy. "Can you guys come too?"

Mandy gulped.

Cassie's mouth dropped open. "Um," she said, "I think I have a dentist appointment."

"On Saturday night?" I asked.

"And I have to clean my room!" Mandy declared.

I rolled my eyes. Mandy hardly *ever* cleaned her room! She and Cassie were just too scared to spend the night at Shelby's house.

"You're both chicken!" I said. I started flapping my elbows up and down like wings. "Bak, bak, baaaaak!"

"Michelle!" Cassie said.

"We are not chicken!" Mandy insisted.

"Then you'll come?" Shelby asked them.

Cassie and Mandy looked at each other. They nodded their heads slowly.

"You promise?" Shelby asked us.

"Sure!" I said. "If our parents say yes."

"Yay!" Shelby cheered. "I never thought anyone would want to sleep over here!"

Cassie, Mandy, and I ate one last cookie each. Then we walked to the door and said good-bye to Shelby. I couldn't wait for her sleepover!

"We'll have a blast!" Shelby told us. "We'll pop popcorn and watch videos and play games. It'll be so much fun! See you at school tomorrow," she said. "Bye!"

I gasped just as Shelby was closing the door. I saw her red hoodie fly off the chair and land on the floor. Then it floated down the hall—all by itself!

What could make it move like that? There was only one thing I could think of—a *ghost*!

Chapter Five

For the rest of the afternoon I tried and tried to think of another way Shelby's hoodie could have moved by itself. I didn't come up with an answer.

Now I was sitting at the dinner table with my whole family. But my mind wasn't on food. It was on ghosts!

"Dad?" D.J. asked. "Why are we eating pumpkin soup, pumpkin rolls, and pumpkin casserole for dinner tonight?"

Dad was an awesome cook. He was also the host of a TV show. It was called *Good Morning San Francisco!*

"I'm trying out some recipes for our Halloween show next week," Dad said. "Pumpkins are tasty, healthy, and a great way to recycle leftover jack-o'-lanterns!"

"Speaking of Halloween," Uncle Joey said, "why do ghosts make such a terrible audience?"

"Uh-oh." Uncle Jesse groaned. "I feel a joke coming on!"

"I don't know, Joey," Aunt Becky said. She poured water into two cups for the twins. "Why do ghosts make a terrible audience?"

"Because they're always *boo*-ing you!" Uncle Joey said. "Get it?"

Everyone laughed. But I wasn't paying much attention. I was still thinking about that red hoodie.

"Michelle?" Uncle Joey cut into my thoughts. "Didn't you think the joke was funny?"

I looked up. "Huh?"

"What's the matter, honey?" Dad asked me. "Are you okay?"

"I'm fine, Dad," I said. Then I heaved a big sigh.

"Hmm," Dad said. "Looks like you're thinking about a serious problem."

"Is it another 'Dear Michelle' letter?" Aunt Becky asked. "Can we help?"

That's when I told them the whole story. About how Shelby was Ghost Girl. And how her hoodie moved by itself. And how her house might really be haunted.

"I didn't believe in ghosts before," I said, "but now maybe I do. What do you think, Dad? Could Shelby's house be haunted?"

Dad smiled and shook his head. "I told you once before, Michelle," he said. "There are no such things as ghosts!"

"Ghosts are only in movies and on TV," D.J. said.

"Like Casper!" Alex chimed in.

"Oh, yeah?" Stephanie asked. She turned to Dad. "Then what about that guy you had on your show? The one who said he could talk to ghosts."

Dad raised an eyebrow. "That doesn't mean there *are* ghosts," he said.

"Are you sure, Dad?" I asked.

"Sure I'm sure," Dad said. "There's got to be a logical reason for Shelby's floating hoodie."

"Like what?" I asked.

Dad shrugged. "Like maybe a breeze from the window blew it off the chair," he said.

"Hey! I think you're right!" I said. "Why didn't I think of that? The door was open when I saw the hoodie move. I bet that's what happened!"

I smiled. My family always made me feel better!

"Dad?" I asked. "Is it okay if I sleep at Shelby's house on Saturday?"

"I'll have to call her mom for the details," Dad said. "But I think it'll be okay."

"Cool!" I cheered. "Shelby will be so happy. It'll be the first sleepover in her new house!"

I ate my pumpkin roll, pumpkin casserole, and pumpkin pie. When we were all finished eating, Stephanie and I helped Dad clear the dishes from the table.

"So where does Shelby live anyway?" Stephanie asked when Dad went into the kitchen.

"She lives at 1515 Hummingbird Lane," I told her.

Stephanie stared at me. Then she stared up at the ceiling. "Ooooh, boy," she said.

"What?" I asked.

"Nothing," Stephanie said. "Never mind."

No way, I thought. Stephanie knows something about Shelby's house, and she isn't telling me!

"Come on, Steph," I said. "Tell me. You have to tell me."

"It's nothing, Michelle. Really," Stephanie said.

"I don't believe you." I grabbed her arm. "Please! *You have to tell me!*"

"Okay, okay." Stephanie finally gave in. "Shelby's house really *is* haunted."

"But you heard what Dad told us," I said. "The wind probably blew her hoodie off the chair."

Stephanie shook her head. "No, Michelle. This has nothing to do with Shelby's hoodie," she said. "This is about the ghost of Albert Dunnigan. A long, long time ago he lived in that house with his wife and kids. But then he had to go to war. Years later, when he came back home, his family was gone. He vowed to stay in that house until they returned. People say he's still there, waiting for them."

I gasped. "Really? What happened to his family?"

Stephanie shrugged. "I don't know. But I *do* know that 1515 Hummingbird Lane is totally ghost central!"

I gulped. The kids at Stephanie's school were twelve, thirteen—even fourteen—years old. They knew practically everything!

Oh, no, I thought. Who do I believe?

Dad or Stephanie?

Chapter Six

"Are you sure, Michelle?" Cassie asked the next morning on the school bus.

"Maybe Stephanie was just joking," Mandy said.

I shook my head. "Uncle Joey jokes," I said. "Stephanie was serious."

I sat next to Mandy. Cassie sat in front of us. I had just told them what Stephanie said about Shelby's house.

Cassie leaned over the back of her seat. "Now I *really* don't want to go to Shelby's sleepover!"

"Me neither," Mandy said. "Telling

ghost stories at sleepovers is cool. Seeing a *real* ghost—not cool!"

The dark green seat squeaked as I sank way back into it. I still didn't know what to think. Was Stephanie right? Was Shelby's house haunted? Or was Dad right? Was there another reason for the moving hoodie? I didn't know the answer, but I did know one thing. . . .

"We have to go to the sleepover," I told Cassie and Mandy. "We promised Shelby. And a promise is a promise."

"But what if we see a ghost?" Mandy asked. "Or hear it, like Shelby does every night?"

Good question, I thought. Then I remembered the ghosts on the Chiller Channel on TV. They never stuck around too long. Somebody always found a way to get rid of them. That gave me an idea!

I sat up straight in my seat. "Cassie,

Mandy, if Shelby's house *is* haunted, we'll know just what to do."

"Run?" Cassie asked.

"No!" I said, shaking my head. "Instead of the ghost scaring us away, we'll scare the ghost away!"

My friends stared at me. Cassie looked worried. Mandy seemed curious.

"How do you get rid of a ghost, Michelle?" Mandy asked.

"Good question," I said. "That's the one teeny thing I have to figure out first. How *do* you scare a ghost?"

"The Chiller Channel will be right back," the TV announcer said. "But *you* might not be. Mwah, hah, hah!"

I lowered the volume with the remote control.

It was Friday afternoon—one day away from Shelby's sleepover. Mandy and I sat on the sofa in the den at my house. We were watching the scariest channel on TV.

But we weren't watching it to get goose bumps. We were trying to get ideas on how to scare a ghost.

Cassie was there too. But she wasn't sitting on the sofa. She was hiding *behind* it!

I stared down at the blank page in the notebook on my lap. "What do we know so far about ghosts?" I asked.

"They're *creepy!*" Cassie yelled from behind the sofa.

"Besides that," I said.

"Once I saw a movie where a ghost was scared away by garlic!" Mandy said. "I think it was called *Children of the Night.*"

I wrote down the word *garlic* in my notebook. "My dad has a can of powdered pizza garlic in the kitchen," I said. "I'll bring it to the sleepover, just in case we need it to scare the ghost."

I heard Cassie whimper.

"Just in case!" I repeated.

Mandy tossed a pillow into the air and caught it. "Garlic is stinky," she said. "So maybe ghosts hate stinky stuff."

"Maybe!" I agreed. "So let's bring lots of stinky stuff to Shelby's sleepover."

"Like what?" Mandy asked.

"Like Uncle Jesse's gym sneakers!" I said. "Even Comet won't go near them!"

"Yuck!" Mandy pointed to my notebook. "Write down *stinky sneakers*, Michelle!"

"Okay!" I added the stinky sneakers to the list. "Maybe we can even sprinkle garlic *inside* the sneakers!"

"Double-yuck!" Mandy cried. She tugged at my sleeve. "Look! The movie is starting again!"

I turned up the volume. We were getting to the really scary part now. A ghost had just taken over a little girl's body. The little girl's eyeballs rolled up in her head and she was walking around the playground in a trance.

"I can't look!" Cassie covered her eyes.

I turned up the volume even more. "You guys?" I asked. "Did you notice that ghosts always show up when there's slow, scary music playing?"

"S-s-so?" Cassie stammered.

"Maybe ghosts hate fast, loud music," I said. "Like D.J. 's favorite group, Toe Jam!"

"Ask D.J. if we can borrow some Toe Jam CDs!" Mandy said.

"Right!" I wrote *Toe Jam CDs* under *garlic* and *stinky sneakers*.

Mandy leaned over the sofa arm. She picked up a cage sitting on the floor. "Hey, Cassie!" she called. "Don't you want to say hi to Swifty?"

Cassie shrieked from behind the sofa.

Mandy snickered. It was her turn to take

home the class gerbil for the weekend. She had been scaring Cassie with it all day.

"I don't know why you're so afraid of a little gerbil," I said to Cassie.

"Because gerbils look like mice," Cassie snapped. "And I'm afraid of mice too!"

"Hmm," I said. That made me think. If Cassie is so scared of Swifty, maybe a ghost would be too.

"Mandy?" I asked. "Can we bring Swifty to the sleepover?"

"Sure!" Mandy said. She checked the gerbil's cage one more time. "Want to come to Shelby's house tomorrow night?"

"No!" Cassie cried from behind the sofa.

I giggled. Cassie could be such a baby sometimes!

I checked my list one more time. "Garlic . . . stinky sneakers . . . Toe Jam CDs . . ." Then I leaned close to Mandy and whispered the last thing. "And gerbil."

"We came up with some cool stuff!" Mandy said. "Didn't we, Michelle?"

"Totally!" I agreed. "Now let's go to that sleepover tomorrow night and show those ghosts we mean business!"

Chapter Seven

"**W**ow!" Shelby said the night of the sleepover. "Is it Halloween already?"

We *must* have looked pretty weird standing on her doorstep.

Mandy was holding Swifty's cage. Cassie and I were wearing special ghost goggles—to protect us against ghosts.

We had cut them out from the backs of cereal boxes. And I was holding a shopping bag filled with the rest of our ghost gear.

"Don't worry, Shelby," I told her. "We brought a few things just in case we see a ghost."

"You mean *when* you see a ghost!" Shelby said. She stepped aside and waved us into the house. "Come on in!"

We followed Shelby into the house. She was wearing a blue T-shirt that read: *I didn't sleep a wink at Shelby's first sleepover!*

"My mom made shirts for all of us!" Shelby said. She squeezed her hands together and grinned. "We are going to have so much fun. We're going to make popcorn and watch videos and braid our hair and—"

"Chase away ghosts," Cassie added.

I nudged Cassie with my elbow.

Mrs. Warner and Rufus were coming over. Rufus was tossing his softball into a catcher's mitt. Mrs. Warner helped us hang our jackets on a brass coatrack in the hall.

Uh-oh, I thought. What if my jacket floats away too? Just like Shelby's hoodie?

I tried not to think about that. Besides, if there was a ghost in this house, we were ready for it. At least I hoped so!

"Let's get this party started!" Shelby said. She led us into the kitchen for a surprise. Her mom had bought everything we needed to make little pizzas!

"There's mozzarella cheese, tomato sauce, and toppings," Mrs. Warner said. "The only thing I forgot to buy is garlic."

"Garlic?" Cassie said. "We have plenty of that in our—"

I clapped a hand over Cassie's mouth. We didn't want Mrs. Warner to know that we were on a ghost hunt. "Who wants that stinky stuff anyway?" I said.

We made tiny pizzas with gobs of tomato sauce, lots of cheese, pepperoni, and olives.

Rufus wanted to add marshmallows, but we all yelled, "Ewwwww!"

After we pigged out, Mrs. Warner took

Rufus up to bed. Then Shelby led us to her bedroom. The walls of her room were painted light blue, and there were white curtains over the window.

We piled our sleeping bags, backpacks, and the ghost gear at the foot of Shelby's bed. Mandy placed Swifty's cage on Shelby's desk.

"So, how do you like my room?" Shelby asked us.

"It's neat!" I said.

Mandy and I sat on Shelby's bed. It was covered with a white bedspread that had a yellow and blue flower design on it. It was so cheerful. Not scary at all.

Cassie stood in the middle of Shelby's blue rug. "Is this where you are when you hear the ghost?" she asked Shelby. She looked around the room with wide eyes.

"Yup," Shelby said. "But I hear it only late at night."

Mandy looked at her pink and purple bubble watch. "Well, it's not late yet," she said. "So let's have as much fun as we can before the ghost shows up."

Shelby's mother brought up a big bowl of popcorn. Then she said she'd be in the attic if we needed her. She had to unpack a few boxes.

Shelby ran to her dresser and picked up a DVD. "Let's watch this!" she said, holding it high. "It's my favorite movie."

"*Monkey Business!*" I cheered. "That's my favorite too!" Even though I'd seen it a million times, it still made me laugh.

After the movie the four of us played three games of Life and four games of Twister.

Then we sat on the rug and braided each other's hair.

"What should we do after this?" Shelby asked.

"I know! Let's call Jeff Farrington and hang up!" Cassie said, laughing.

We all giggled as we braided. Then I heard a noise.

Thump . . . Thump . . .

Shelby yanked on my hair.

"Ow!" I yelped.

"Listen!" Shelby whispered. "There it is!"

"Oh, noooo!" Cassie moaned.

Thump . . . Thump . . .

"That's the sound I hear almost every night!" Shelby said. She started to shake. "That's the ghost, Michelle!"

"Uh-oh," Mandy said. "What are we going to do?"

I gulped. "You guys?" I said slowly. "Remember when I said that the ghost gear was for *just in case* there was a ghost?"

"Yes," Mandy said.

"Well, just in case is—*now*!" I said.

We all jumped up. I raced to the bag of ghost gear and pulled out our first secret weapon—the can of powdered garlic!

"Stand back!" I warned as I popped off the lid. I sprinkled the smelly stuff around Shelby's room.

"Michelle, what are you doing?" Shelby asked. She squeezed her nose. "That stuff stinks!"

"Mandy saw a creepy movie once," I said, still sprinkling, "where a ghost was scared away by garlic!"

"Yeah!" Mandy said. "It was called *Children of the Night.*"

"*Children of the Night*?" Shelby repeated. "I saw that movie too. The garlic wasn't for ghosts. It was for vampires!"

Thump . . . Thump . . . Thump!

"Oh, no!" I jumped back and dropped the can. "Are you sure garlic doesn't scare ghosts?" I asked.

Thump . . . Thump . . . Thump!

"Of course I'm sure," Shelby said. "Garlic is definitely used to scare vampires. Not ghosts."

Thump . . . Thump . . . THUMP!

"The ghost is getting closer!" I said.

THUMP! THUMP! THUMP!

"Oh, no!" I shivered. "I think it's in the room with us right now!"

Chapter Eight

We huddled in the middle of Shelby's room.

"Do you really think the ghost is here with us?" Shelby shivered.

"You can't always see ghosts," Mandy whispered.

"And they can walk through walls," I said. "That's what makes them ghosts! So let's get the rest of our ghost gear—and scare the ghost out of here!"

"I'll grab Swifty," Mandy said.

"I'll play Toe Jam," Cassie said.

"I'll get Uncle Jesse's stinky sneakers!" I said.

Unscramble the words
to get a secret
message from
Michelle!

YPAPH
UPKNPMI
AYD!

Write the unscrambled message here.

Dear Michelle
c/o HarperEntertainment
10 East 53rd Street
New York, NY 10022

"I'll put on the ghost goggles!" Shelby said.

Cassie and I ran to get the bag of ghost gear. Mandy lifted Swifty out of his cage. Shelby pulled on the ghost goggles.

"Ghost, go away!" Mandy held Swifty out in front of her. "And don't come back!"

"Take a sniff!" I waved the sneakers. "And go back where you came from!"

Cassie was about to slip the CD into Shelby's boom box when we all heard an extra loud *THUMP!*

The noise made us jump. And it made Swifty leap right out of Mandy's hands!

Squeeeeeeeak!

"Swifty, come back!" Mandy called as the gerbil scurried around Shelby's room.

"That's was the loudest thump so far," I said. "It sounds as if it came from the hallway!"

"That's great," Shelby said. "It means the ghost isn't in the room with us, right?"

"Thank goodness!" Cassie sighed.

"Maybe," I said. But I had to see for myself. I walked to the door. I opened it slowly. I peeked into the hall—and gasped.

Moving along the wall was a tall, dark shadow. It was coming straight toward us!

"Yikes!" I slammed the door shut.

"What is it?" Cassie cried.

"The ghost!" I cried, leaning on the door.

"I knew it! I knew it!" Shelby said.

"I'm never leaving this room!" Cassie said. "Never ever!"

"Me neither," Mandy said. "No matter what!"

I didn't want to go out there either.

I saw something out in the hall that no one else saw.

"You guys," I said. "We have to go out there."

"No way!" Cassie cried.

"We have to," I said. "And here's why. . . ."

Chapter Nine

"Why do we have to go out there?" Mandy asked.

"Well." I gulped. "When I opened Shelby's bedroom door, Swifty ran into the hall."

"Oh, no." Mandy groaned. "It was my turn to take care of him this weekend," she said. "Mrs. Ramirez will be so angry when she finds out I lost him!"

"What will the ghost do to poor Swifty?" Shelby asked.

Aunt Becky once taught me how to stay calm. Just take a deep, deep breath, I told myself. So I did.

"There's only one thing to do." I pointed to the door. "We have to go out there and save Swifty."

"How?" Shelby finally asked.

"We'll take our ghost stuff," I told her. "I'll take the stinky sneakers."

"And we can carry the boom box with us," Mandy added. "And play Toe Jam!"

Shelby wore the ghost goggles. Mandy carried the boom box. Cassie held one of Uncle Jesse's sneakers. I held the other.

"We're ready for action," I said. "Now let's go out there and save our class pet!"

I opened the door slowly. The tall dark shadow on the wall was gone. "Let's go," I whispered.

We walked out of the room carefully and quietly. We stood in the hall and looked around.

No sign of Swifty.

"H-h-he's probably downstairs," I said

in a shaky voice. "So we have to go down-stairs too."

"But what if the ghost is down there?" Shelby asked.

"Then we'll *stink* him out!" Cassie declared. She raised Uncle Jesse's sneaker in the air.

Wow, I thought. Cassie is getting brave!

That made me feel brave too. So I led the way down the stairs. Lucky for us Mrs. Warner left night-lights on throughout the house.

As we neared the stairs Mandy grabbed my arm. "Listen!" she whispered. "I hear something downstairs."

I held my breath and listened. I heard a man's voice, then some music. "It sounds like the TV," I said. "And the radio."

"I told you," Shelby said. "I hear that almost every night. And it's *not* my mom."

Now I was really scared.

Everything Shelby said would happen *is* happening, I thought. First we heard the thumping noise in her bedroom. And now the TV and the radio!

"The ghost is watching TV," Mandy said. "We can't go down there!"

"We have to," I whispered. "How else are we going to save Swifty?"

We inched our way down the stairs. The TV in the den was on, but no one was watching.

We headed into the kitchen. The radio was on, but no one was listening. And the refrigerator door was swinging wide open!

"Looks like he's a hungry ghost," Shelby said. She shut the refrigerator door.

"Let's just hope he doesn't eat gerbils," Mandy said.

THUMP . . . THUMP . . . THUMP!

Everyone froze.

"It sounds like it's coming from the dining room," Shelby said.

SQUEEEEEEEEEAK!

That noise came from the dining room too. "Oh, no!" I cried. "It's Swifty!"

Chapter Ten

We huddled outside the dining room door.

"Who is going in there first?" I asked.

Everyone pointed at *me*.

No fair! I was scared too! "Why don't we count to three instead?" I said. "Then we'll *all* run in at the same time."

My friends nodded. We started to count. "One . . . two . . ."

SQUEEEEEEEEEEEAK!

I gave a little shriek. Something furry ran out of the dining room. And right between my legs!

"Swifty!" I scooped up the little gerbil.

We were all happy to see him. Even Cassie!

"Let's get out of here!" I said.

As we turned around I heard a voice, "I want a puppy. . . . You take the licorice jelly bean. . . . That's my purple crayon. . . ."

I looked back at my friends. Who was that?

Slowly we peeked into the dining room. Standing in the middle of the room was Shelby's little brother Rufus!

A blue blanket hung over his shoulders. He was wearing a catcher's mitt on one hand and holding a chicken leg in the other.

"Rufus!" Shelby called. "What are you doing down here? There's a ghost in the house!"

Rufus didn't move. He just stared ahead with a weird grin on his face. "I know. . . ."

69

"Come on," Shelby said. "Run!"

"I don't want to go to the dentist. . . . My sister likes peanut-butter-and-pickle sandwiches. . . ." Rufus said.

"Since when?" Mandy asked Shelby.

"I don't!" Shelby cried. She turned to us and waved her arms. "I don't know why my brother is acting so weird!"

I stared at Rufus. His eyes were wide open, but he didn't seem to be looking at anything! "It's strange," I said. "It's as if Rufus is in some kind of . . . trance!"

"Trance?" Cassie gasped. "It-it-it's just like that movie on the Chiller Channel!"

I remembered that movie. And what the ghost did to that poor little girl!

"Oh, no!" I cried. "The ghost took over Rufus's body!"

Chapter Eleven

Shelby yanked off her ghost goggles and screamed, "My little brother is a zombie!"

All four of us shrieked.

"Girls, girls!" Mrs. Warner called out. "What's going on down here?"

I spun around. Shelby's mom had come downstairs. She was tying the belt to her pink robe around her waist.

"What happened?" Mrs. Warner asked. She looked at her son. "What's Rufus doing down here?"

Shelby, Cassie, Mandy, and I ran over to Mrs. Warner.

"Mom!" Shelby said. "There's a ghost in Rufus's body!"

"A ghost?" Mrs. Warner asked.

We all started talking at once:

"We heard this thumping noise!"

"And the TV downstairs!"

"The radio too!"

THUMP!

Everyone whirled around. Rufus's softball fell out of his mitt. He slowly bent to pick it up. He put it back in his mitt.

THUMP!

He dropped it again.

I stared at the ball on the carpet. Could that have made the thumping noise?

"Marshmallows . . . pizza muffins," Rufus mumbled. He bent down again, picked up his softball, and tucked it back into his mitt.

THUMP!

This time, Rufus left the ball on the floor. We watched Rufus as he walked right past us. He handed Shelby his chewed up chicken leg. Then he left the living room.

"Where is he going?" Shelby asked.

We followed Rufus down the hall and into the den. First he turned off the TV. Then he walked into the kitchen and turned off the radio.

"You see, Mom?" Shelby tossed the chicken bone into the trash can. "Rufus doesn't know what he's doing. He even said I liked peanut-butter-and-pickle sandwiches!"

Rufus walked to the open refrigerator. The blue blanket fell off his shoulders as he leaned in to take a look.

Mrs. Warner watched Rufus very closely. "Don't worry, girls," she finally said. "Rufus wasn't taken over by a ghost."

"Then what's wrong with him?" I asked.

"It looks as if he's sleepwalking," Mrs. Warner said. She walked to Rufus and put her hands on his shoulders. "Rufus. Wake up, honey. Wake up."

Rufus pulled his head out of the refrigerator. He blinked a couple of times. Then he looked at his mother.

"I had a dream we were in our old house, Mom," Rufus said. He glanced around the kitchen. "What am I doing down here?" he asked.

"It's okay, Rufus," Mrs. Warner said gently. "I'll explain everything to you tomorrow."

"I don't get it," I said. "How can Rufus do all that stuff while he's still asleep?"

"Sleepwalkers can do just about anything they can do while they're awake," Mrs. Warner explained. "They can turn on the TV. And open the refrigerator. And sometimes even talk to you."

"Wow!" Mandy exclaimed.

"I've never met a sleepwalker before," Cassie said.

Mrs. Warner put her arm around Rufus's shoulders.

"So all those noises I heard during the night weren't ghosts?" Shelby asked. "They were . . . Rufus?"

Mrs. Warner nodded.

"And your house *isn't* haunted?" Cassie asked.

"No," Mrs. Warner said with a grin. "The thumping noise you heard was probably Rufus dropping his softball."

"All right!" I cheered. "There are no such thing as ghosts! I was right!"

I felt Mandy tap my shoulder. "Oh, yeah?" she said. "Then what's that?"

I looked to see where Mandy was pointing. The blue blanket that had been wearing around Rufus around his shoulders was now moving across the floor.

"Oh, no!" I said. "Not again!"

Chapter Twelve

"The ghost is back!" Cassie cried.

My heart raced. I watched the blue blanket move slowly across the floor. Just like Shelby's red hoodie had!

"You guys!" Shelby laughed. She shook her head as she walked to the blue blanket. "That's not a ghost!"

"Then what is it?" Mandy asked.

Shelby pulled up the blanket. "It's Inky!"

MEOW!

We stared at the black cat. He stared back at us with big green eyes.

"Inky?" I asked.

Rufus laughed and said, "He likes to crawl under stuff."

Shelby nodded. "Like blankets, towels—"

"Hoodies?" I asked.

"Sure," Shelby said with a shrug. "I guess he could crawl under a hoodie too."

Inky padded over to me. He looked up at Swifty and hissed.

"Uh-oh." I held Swifty close to my chest. "Time for this pet to go back into his cage!"

"And it's time for you girls to go to sleep," Mrs. Warner said. "That's why they call them *sleep*overs!"

I *was* getting sleepy. Chasing a ghost that wasn't a ghost was hard work!

"By the way," Mrs. Warner said, sniffing the air. "What's that awful smell?"

Cassie hid Uncle Jesse's sneakers behind her back. "What smell?" she asked.

Mandy and I giggled. We would tell Mrs. Warner all about our ghost adventure tomorrow.

"'The Spider in the School Lunchroom,' by Lucas Hamilton!" Lucas held up the front page of the *Third-Grade Buzz*. "I'm the man! I'm the man!" he cheered.

It was Monday morning, and Mrs. Ramirez was passing out copies of the first issue of our brand-new newspaper. It was on bright orange paper with black type. Perfect for Halloween!

"All right!" Bailey said when she saw her sports column.

Sergei seemed proud of his story called "I Like America."

But Paige looked disappointed. "My drawings are in the newspaper," she said. "But they're not pink. I wanted them all to be pink!"

"Pink?" Julia rolled her eyes. "Whoever heard of a *pink* jack-o'-lantern?"

Jeff tilted his head all the way to one side. "I think there's a mistake," he said, holding up his copy of the paper. "The answer to my riddle is upside down."

"That's not a mistake," Mrs. Ramirez said. "When our readers finish guessing your riddle, they'll flip the paper upside down for the answer."

Then Mrs. Ramirez grinned as she handed me my own copy. I was too excited to open it!

"Go ahead, Michelle," Mandy said.

"Yeah," Cassie said. "I want to see your very first 'Dear Michelle' column!"

"Okay, okay." I tried hard to stay calm. "I'll count to three. Then I'll open it!"

Cassie, Mandy, Shelby, and Elizabeth stood around me as I counted, "One . . . two . . . three!" I quickly flipped it open. I found the words *Dear Michelle* at the top of the third page! "Ta-da!" I held the paper up high.

"You're famous, Michelle!" Cassie said.

"May I have your autograph?" Mandy joked. She pretended to beg. "Please? I'll be your best friend!"

"Me too!" Cassie joined in.

"You guys already *are* my best friends." I giggled. "And I don't really care if I'm famous or not."

"*I* do!" Shelby declared. She turned to the class and shouted, "Hey, everybody—I'm Ghost Girl!"

Shelby smiled as our classmates crowded around to hear her story about the ghost that wasn't a ghost.

I smiled too and headed to my desk. I tipped over my letter box. This time *tons* of letters spilled out onto my desk!

I couldn't wait to read them!

Hi, I'm Michelle Tanner!

I get lots of letters. That's because I write the advice column for my class newspaper, the Third-Grade Buzz. I learned in school that a good letter has five special parts. Do you want to know how to write a good letter? Then check out the one on the next page and learn about the five special parts too. But watch out! I added a sixth part!

Six Special Parts for Writing a Good Letter:

(1) October 13

(2) Dear Michelle,

(3) I don't know what to wear for my Halloween costume. I was planning to wear a kitten costume. But my big sister says that's for babies. Should I wear the kitten costume or not?

(4) I can't wait for your answer!

(5) Sincerely,
Bailey

(6) PS: If I don't wear the kitten costume, what should I wear?

(1) The date. The day you write the letter.

(2) How you start a letter. Bailey put my name here because she wrote the letter to me.

(3) The body of a letter. This is what Bailey wanted to tell me.

(4) Bailey is getting ready to end the letter here.

(5) The closing of a letter. Bailey signed her name.

(6) Oops! Bailey forgot to ask me something, so she added it here. That's the sixth part.

Now that you know the parts of a letter,
use the space below to help me write
an answer to Bailey's letter!

_____
Date

Dear Bailey,

_____

_____

_____

_____

_____

_____

_____

_____

_____

_____

_____

_____

Do you need some advice—or want to ask me a question? I may be able to answer you in one of my future columns! I wish I could answer all of your letters, but I get too many! I would still love to hear from you. Write to me, Michelle, at:

Dear Michelle
c/o HarperEntertainment
10 East 53rd Street
New York, NY 10022

You can use the cool postcard in this book. It already has the address on it!

Full House Dear MICHELLE

#2 How Will Santa Find Me?

The recess bell rang and the class lined up by the door.

Louie Rizzoli tapped me on the shoulder. He shoved a piece of gum into his mouth.

"What's up, Louie?" I asked.

Louie's gum smelled like bananas. He blew a bubble and it popped over his whole face!

"Are you sure about the answer to your last letter?" Louie asked. He scraped some gum off his nose. "The one about the kid who is going away for Chistmas?"

I glanced at Cassie and Mandy as the line moved out of the classroom. Then I told Louie, "Yes, I'm sure."

Mandy raised an eyebrow at me. She and Cassie knew that I *wasn't* sure if Santa would find Been Really Good in Colorado. I wasn't even sure if Santa would find me at my grandma's house in Connecticut.

"Well, maybe I'm not totally sure," I added.

Louie's whole face drooped. "I knew it!" he said. "I just knew it!"

Mrs. Ramirez led us out of the classroom and into the school yard.

Louie marched over to the monkey bars. Mandy, Cassie, and I followed him.

"Why do you care so much about my answer anyway," I asked Louie.

Louie leaned against the monkey bars. "Because I'm the kid who wrote the letter," he said. "I'm Been Really Good. And I bet I won't get anything for Christmas this year!"

Louie's bubblegum dropped out of his

open mouth when he said *Christmas*. We jumped aside as it plopped onto the ground in front of us.

"Gross!" Cassie cried.

"How can you be Been Really Good, Louie?" Mandy asked. "You stuck gum on my chair just last week!"

"Yeah, but since then I've been really good," Louie said. "I promise! You can ask my sister!"

"Listen, Louie," I told him. "You're not the only one going away for Christmas. I am too!"

Louie stared at me. "You are?"

"I'm going to my grandma's house in Connecticut!" I said. "So Santa may not find me on Christmas either!"

Louie heaved a big sigh. "What are we going to do?" he asked. "It's not as if we can just *tell* Santa where we'll be."

Tell Santa? Louie didn't know it, but he

just gave me an awesome idea!

"Hey, Louie! Why *can't* we tell Santa?" I asked with a big smile.

"What do you mean?" Louie asked. "How?"

"I bet we can figure out a good way to let Santa know where we'll be for Christmas—if we do it together," I said.

"You mean like a team?" Louie smiled.

"Hey, Michelle!" Mandy said. "Can I help?"

"I want to help too!" Cassie added quickly.

"Sure!" I told them. "Santa has helpers. Why shouldn't we?" I turned back to Louie. "So, is it a deal?"

Louie nodded. "You bet!" he said. "How do we start?"

Check out these other great

titles

Coming Soon!

How Will Santa Find Me?

Who Will Be My Valentine?

I've Got Bunny Business!